LONE HAWK

THE STORY OF AIR ACE BILLY BISHOP

A GRAPHIC NOVEL BY JOHN LANG

PUFFIN
CANADA

PUFFIN CANADA

Published by the Penguin Group

Penguin Group (Canada), 90 Eglinton Avenue East, Suite 700, Toronto, Ontario,
Canada M4P 2Y3 (a division of Pearson Canada Inc.)
Penguin Group (USA) Inc., 375 Hudson Street, New York, New York 10014, U.S.A.
Penguin Books Ltd, 80 Strand, London WC2R 0RL, England
Penguin Ireland, 25 St Stephen's Green, Dublin 2, Ireland
(a division of Penguin Books Ltd)
Penguin Group (Australia), 250 Camberwell Road, Camberwell, Victoria 3124,
Australia (a division of Pearson Australia Group Pty Ltd)
Penguin Books India Pvt Ltd, 11 Community Centre, Panchsheel Park,
New Delhi – 110 017, India
Penguin Group (NZ), 67 Apollo Drive, Rosedale, Auckland 0632,
New Zealand (a division of Pearson New Zealand Ltd)
Penguin Books (South Africa) (Pty) Ltd, 24 Sturdee Avenue, Rosebank,
Johannesburg 2196, South Africa

Penguin Books Ltd, Registered Offices: 80 Strand, London WC2R 0RL, England

First published 2011

1 2 3 4 5 6 7 8 9 10 (WEB)

Copyright © John Lang, 2011

Manufactured in Canada

Library and Archives Canada Cataloguing in Publication

Lang, John, 1983-
Lone hawk : the story of air ace Billy Bishop / John Lang.

ISBN 978-0-14-317466-0

1. Bishop, William A., 1894–1956—Comic books, strips, etc. 2. Bishop, William A.,
1894–1956—Juvenile literature. 3. Fighter pilots—Canada—Biography—Comic
books, strips, etc. 4. Fighter pilots—Canada—Biography—Juvenile literature.
5. Great Britain. Royal Flying Corps—Biography—Comic books, strips, etc.
6. Great Britain. Royal Flying Corps—Biography—Juvenile literature. 7. World
War, 1914–1918—Aerial operations, British—Comic books, strips, etc. 8. World
War, 1914–1918—Aerial operations, British—Juvenile literature. I. Title.

UG626.2.B5L35 2011   j940.4'4941092   C2011-902081-5

Visit the Penguin Group (Canada) website at **www.penguin.ca**

Special and corporate bulk purchase rates available; please see
www.penguin.ca/corporatesales or call 1-800-810-3104, ext. 2477

For my dad, whose love of aviation inspired me to tell this story.

FOREWORD
By Jeff Lemire

I was never much of a history buff. I loved stories ... but mostly the fictional kind. Myths, legends ... especially the four-colored kind that featured superheroes. So rather than pay any attention to my teachers I spent most of my school days either doodling such things in the margins of my notebooks or flat out hiding comic books inside my textbooks during class. But, if I had taken my head out of my comic books for just a second, I may have noticed that the stories we were being taught, the real life adventures of such great Canadians as Louis Riel and Billy Bishop, were every bit as fantastic and enjoyable as Batman and Superman's latest caper. Unlike me, John Lang must have taken the time to listen.

As far as debut graphic novels go, *Lone Hawk* is winner. Lang fully understands and employs the strengths of the comics' medium to build a concise portrait of one of those aforementioned real-life Canadian heroes, Billy Bishop. The clarity of John's art style bears particular mention. My own drawing style's been called everything from scratchy to expressive to downright sloppy, so no one is ever going to mistake my work with John's. But his clear line work perfectly suits the story of Billy Bishop, and makes his tale particularly accessible and "real." Each panel is like a snapshot from the past, giving the reader a window into history and the exciting story of one of our nation's greatest war heroes.

Equally as interesting is Lang's portrait of the man himself. On the surface his Bishop is stoic and noble, but from the opening scene we get the sense that there is a fire burning in the belly of this boy named Billy from Owen Sound … something special driving him to become the man we all know as Canada's greatest fighter pilot. Again, Lang's square-jawed character design and attention to detail captures this perfectly.

Talking about art style and character design is great, but all of that is only a part of what makes a successful graphic novel. In other words, the aesthetics are great, but mean very little if the storytelling itself falls flat. Well, Billy Bishop had a great story, and it's one that John's widescreen storytelling and cinematic pacing captures perfectly. In fact it's John's accessible storytelling that may be *Lone Hawk*'s greatest strength. This is a book that can be enjoyed and appreciated by young and old readers alike and that's great. But maybe even more importantly it can also be appreciated by fans of graphic novels and newcomers to this great medium John and I both know and love.

Lone Hawk is a great historical account of an important Canadian, and that's great, but at its core it's also a really good story, told well by a cartoonist who is still only at the beginning of what will undoubtedly be a long and exciting career. A few more books like this and kids won't have to hide their comic books inside their textbooks much longer; their comics *will be* their textbooks!

"IF HE'S *LUCKY,* HE MIGHT HIT ONE OR TWO."

click

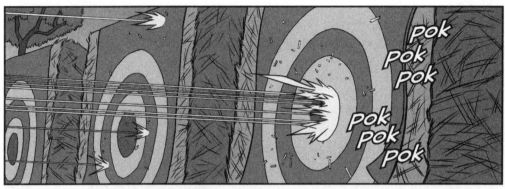

THAT'S SOME DAMN IMPRESSIVE SHOOTING, BISHOP.

YOU MIGHT JUST BE ABLE TO WIN THE WAR ON YOUR *OWN.*

THANK YOU, SIR.

I'LL SHOW THE GERMANS WHAT I'VE GOT-- IF I EVER GET THE *CHANCE.*

LIEUTENANT BISHOP, SIR?

HELLO, GEORGE!

WHAT CAN I DO FOR YOU?

JUNE, 1915
LONDON, ONTARIO

7TH CANADIAN MOUNTED RIFLES CAVALRY CAMP

WELL, SIR--

YOU CAN CALL ME *BISH*, GEORGE.

ALL RIGHT-- BISH.

I JUST WANTED TO THANK YOU FOR SHOWING ME AROUND THE OTHER DAY...

...ME BEING NEW TO THE *CAVALRY CAMP* AND ALL.

NO THANKS NECESSARY...

...I'M *BORED STIFF.*

I'M READY FOR SOME *ACTION*--NOT JUST *WAITING* TO BE SENT OVERSEAS, YOU KNOW?

CAN I ASK YOU SOMETHING, BISH?

SHOOT.

HOW DID YOU GET TO BE AN *OFFICER* SO QUICKLY?

YOU'RE A FAIR BIT YOUNGER THAN THE OTHER FELLAS.

FAIR QUESTION, GEORGE.

AS SOON AS GREAT BRITAIN DECLARED WAR ON GERMANY LAST SUMMER, I SIGNED UP FOR DUTY.

THEY WERE DESPERATE FOR RECRUITS WITH *ANY* MILITARY EXPERIENCE...

THREE WEEKS LATER ...

SHORNECLIFF CAVALRY CAMP

NEAR FOLKSTONE, ENGLAND

IS IT AS GLORIOUS AS YOU HOPED, BISH?

...THE BARRACKS ARE NO PALACE, BUT BETTER THAN SLEEPING WITH THE RATS IN THE *TRENCHES,* EH MATE?

YOU SAID IT!

SEEMS LIKE WE'VE GOT IT PRETTY GOOD AROUND HERE--VERY *RELAXED.*

IT'S *GOTTA* BE TO MAKE UP FOR THE *HELL* YOU GO THROUGH IN THE AIR.

YOU MUST BE *BILLY BISHOP*-- ONE OF THE NEW PILOTS.

BISH, THIS IS CORPORAL *WALTER BOURNE*-- YOUR NEW AIRCRAFT MECHANIC.

HE'S A GOOD MAN AND HIS LUCK MIGHT RUB OFF ON YOU--HE ALSO WORKED WITH *ALBERT BALL.*

OH, WHAT A *TALENT* THAT BOY WAS!

NINETEEN YEARS OLD--WON THE MILITARY CROSS, DISTINGUISHED SERVICE ORDER, AND NOW HE'S UP TO *THIRTY* VICTORIES.

MARK MY WORDS, HE'S ON TRACK TO WIN THE *VICTORIA CROSS*-- OUR HIGHEST HONOUR.

...OF COURSE, WHEN HE'D COME HOME, HIS MACHINE WOULD LOOK LIKE A *SIEVE.*

SPEAKING OF WHICH, YOU READY TO SEE WHAT YOU'LL BE *FLYING,* BISH?

...BUT I MIGHT AS WELL ENJOY THE RIDE.

WAIT...

...HUNS!

TOWNESEND IS TELLING ME TO STAY IN FORMATION...

MAJOR SCOTT MUST BE SETTING A *TRAP!*

ALMOST...

...A LITTLE CLOSER...

...NOW!

FWOOSH

R.F.C. HEADQUARTERS

FILESCAMP FARM

WELL, BISH, AFTER THE *TWO DAY* WALK HOME, I'M SURE YOU'RE READY FOR GOOD NEWS.

YOU'VE BEEN CREDITED WITH YOUR FIRST *OFFICIAL VICTORY!*

THE GENERAL HAS SENT WORD THAT YOU'RE TO STAY ON THE FRONT AND OFFERS HIS *CONGRATULATIONS.*

WE'RE LETTING YOU TAKE THE *LEAD* ON THE NEXT PATROL.

...SIR?

SHOOTING DOWN AN ENEMY PLANE IS *EXTREMELY DIFFICULT*, BISH.

MANY OF OUR VETERANS HAVE *NO* VICTORIES AT ALL.

YOU BROUGHT DOWN A HUN IN YOUR *FIRST* DOGFIGHT.

THAT'S AN *INCREDIBLE* FEAT, YOUNG MAN.

NOW-- TAKE A *LOAD OFF*, MATE.

I'M SURE BINNIE'S RIGHT...

...BUT I'M ABOUT TO *LEAD* FIVE FELLOW PILOTS BACK INTO ENEMY TERRITORY.

THE PRESSURE *ALONE* SHOULD BE ENOUGH TO KEEP MY MIND OFF THE PAIN...

...BUT I THINK I CAN *HANDLE IT.*

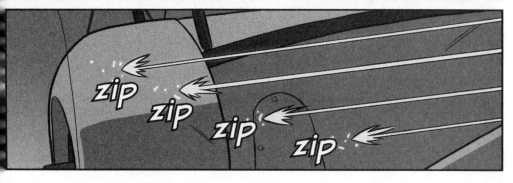

LATER...

R.F.C. HEAD-QUARTERS FILESCAMP FARM

YOU'RE *KEEPING* ME AS FLIGHT LEADER?

I'VE SUBMITTED YOUR MISSION REPORT.

THE BRASS HATS THINK YOU PUT ON A BRILLIANT SHOW.

JACK, I LOST *FOUR* PILOTS...

THAT'S THE BUSINESS WE'RE *IN,* BISH.

YOU BROUGHT DOWN ANOTHER GERMAN MACHINE...

...AND THE OFFENSIVE *MUST* BE MAINTAINED-- EVEN IN THE FACE OF SUBSTANTIAL LOSSES.

THE R.F.C. HAS LOST 75 PLANES IN THE LAST *FIVE DAYS.*

NOW I UNDERSTAND THAT YOU'RE UPSET, BUT I NEED YOU READY FOR ANOTHER MISSION.

THE ALLIES' *BIG PUSH* OF THE SPRING IS STARTING IN A FEW DAYS.

THEY'RE PLANNING ON TAKING *VIMY RIDGE,* AND THEY NEED US TO *CLEAR THE AIR* FOR THEM BEFORE THE BATTLE.

YOU'RE GOING AFTER A GERMAN *OBSERVATION BALLOON.*

IT'S VERY DANGEROUS WORK-- TO BE HONEST, I HATE TO *RISK* YOU ON IT, WHAT WITH YOUR OBVIOUS *TALENT.*

BUT IT HAS TO BE DONE AND ORDERS ARE FOR *ALL* NEW PILOTS TO TAKE THEIR TURN.

YOU'RE UP.

"HANGING THERE AHEAD OF ME--A BIG, BLOATED, *FLYING SAUSAGE.*"

"I START CIRCLING, THEN MOVE IN TO *ATTACK.*"

BUT BEFORE I CAN GET TO IT, I NOTICE THAT *TRACERS* ARE HITTING MY WINGS!

SO I PULL MY NOSE UP-- AND THE HUN FLIES UNDERNEITH AND RIGHT INTO MY *SIGHTS...*

"NEEDLESS TO SAY--THE DEVIL WENT *DOWN.*"

I WAS SOON FREE TO FLY WHEN I WISHED, AND BEGAN MAKING FREQUENT *SOLO PATROLS.*

I PERFECTED MY *TECHNIQUE,* ENSURING THE ELEMENT OF SURPRISE.

SOMETIMES I'D USE THE GLARE OF THE *SUN* TO HELP GAIN THE ADVANTAGE.

IT WAS *FAIR HUNTING*--AND THAT MUCH LESS MISERY THE HUNS COULD BRING.

IF A PATROL WAS SUCCESSFUL, I'D FIRE MY FLARE GUN WHEN I RETURNED.

SOME OF THE OTHERS STARTED CALLING ME *"THE LONE HAWK."*

SOON, I'D HAVE *TWENTY VICTORIES* TO MY NAME.

THE HUNS, UNFORTUNATELY, FARED *BETTER.*

AS *"BLOODY APRIL"* CAME TO A CLOSE, *316* R.F.C. AIRMEN HAD BEEN KILLED.

BEFORE IT WAS OVER, *CAPTAIN ALAN BINNIE* WAS SHOT DOWN BY THE RED BARON'S FLYING CIRCUS.

MAY 6, 1917

R.F.C. HEAD-
QUARTERS
FILESCAMP
FARM

WELL, BISH, *CONGRATULATIONS* ARE IN ORDER...

...YOU'VE WON YOUR FIRST *MEDAL*, THE *MILITARY CROSS*, FOR YOUR ATTACK ON THE GERMAN OBSERVATION BALLOON.

THAT'S GREAT, JACK!

HOWEVER...

...THERE'S A *PROBLEM* WITH YOUR MOST RECENT COMBAT REPORT.

PILOT: ~~LT.~~ Capt. ~~W.A. BISH~~

LOOKS LIKE YOU'RE BUYING *TWICE* THE DRINKS TONIGHT...

...CAPTAIN.

LATER...

FILESCAMP MESS HALL

"CAPTAIN BILLY BISHOP, M.C."

PRETTY SWANKY, MATE!

IT'S NOT *BAD*--BUT WE'LL SEE IF I CAN'T ADD A FEW MORE *LETTERS* TO THAT.

OH, *BUGGER OFF*, BISH!

IF YOU REALLY WANT THE *VICTORIA CROSS*, I'M SURE THE HUNS WILL OBLIGE...

...AIRMEN TEND TO WIN IT *POST-HUMOUSLY!*

WATCH IT, GRID-- YOU DON'T *OUTRANK* ME ANYMORE!

HEY...

...WHERE'S EVERYONE *GOING?*

WELL I'LL BE DAMNED...

THAT'S SOME *MACHINE* YOU'VE GOT OUT THERE.

IT'S THE ROYAL AIRCRAFT FACTORY'S NEW *SE5*--THEY GAVE ME THE FIRST ONE OFF THE LINE.

SHE HAS *TWO GUNS* AND THE *SPEED* TO CATCH AN ALBATROS...

...BUT THAT'S NOT WHY I'M *HERE*.

I HAVE A *PLAN*-- SOMETHING SPECIAL FOR *RICHTHOFEN'S FLYING CIRCUS.*

IT'S *NEVER* BEEN DONE BEFORE, SO THEY WON'T BE *EXPECTING* IT...

BUT IT WILL BE VERY DANGEROUS...

...WHICH IS WHY I'VE COME TO ASK YOU FOR YOUR *HELP,* BISH.

ALL RIGHT-- YOU'VE PIQUED MY *CURIOSITY.*

AT FIRST LIGHT, WHEN THE HUNS' PLANES COME OUT OF THEIR HANGARS...

...*WE ATTACK JASTA 11'S AERODROME.*

CATCH THE PLANES ON THE *GROUND--BEFORE* THEY CAN TAKE OFF.

I'M *IN.*

BUT IT WILL HAVE TO WAIT--I'M GOING ON LEAVE TO ENGLAND IN A FEW DAYS.

WHEN I GET *BACK...*

...*YOU AND I* WILL SHOW THE HUNS WHAT WE'VE *REALLY* GOT.

BISH-- EVEN *BALL* WOULDN'T DO IT ALONE...

...AND *HE* WAS GOING A BIT *BATTY*...

YOU'RE WELCOME TO *JOIN* ME, GRID.

IT'S *MADNESS*, MATE!

EVEN IF CONDITIONS WERE *PERFECT*, YOU'D STILL BE TAKING A *HUGE* RISK!

OR WORSE, IF THERE'S NO *WIND*, THE HUNS'D BE ABLE TO PUT *MULTIPLE PLANES* IN THE AIR IN *ANY* DIRECTION...

...YOU'D BE *TRAPPED!*

GRID'S RIGHT--IT'S NOT *WORTH* IT, BISH!

EARLY CALL CAPT. BISHOP 3 AM

THE NEXT MORNING...

JUNE 2, 1917

JASTA 11'S AERODROME WILL HAVE *LONG-RANGE* MACHINE GUNS...

...I'LL HAVE TO GO IN *LOW*, AT THE TREE LINE.

I'M *WELL* PAST THE GERMAN LINES--IT SHOULD BE COMING UP...

...GET *READY*...

...*NO!*

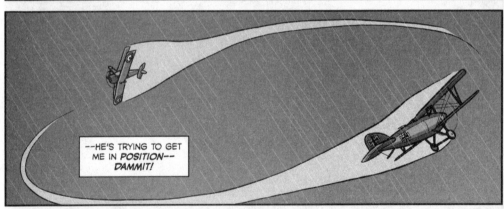

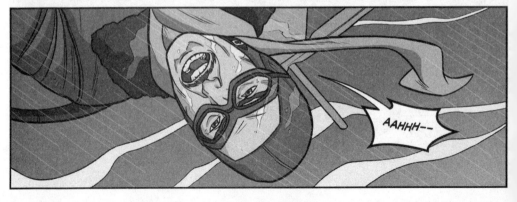

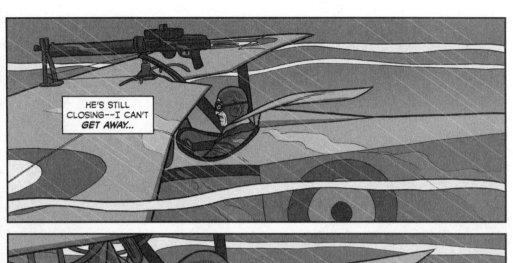

HAVING BEEN GRANTED LEAVE TO *CANADA*, I SOON FOUND THINGS TO BE EQUALLY *STRANGE* AT HOME.

THE NEWSPAPERS HAD PRINTED STORIES OF MY EXPLOITS, AND I WAS HERALDED AS A *WAR HERO.*

WHEN I RETURNED TO OWEN SOUND, *THOUSANDS* OF PEOPLE LINED UP TO CHEER AT MY ARRIVAL.

THIS WAS ONLY MY *FIRST STOP*--THE CANADIAN GOVERNMENT HAD ORGANIZED A *SPEAKING TOUR* FOR ME.

SUPPORT FOR THE WAR WAS *WANING* AND THEY THOUGHT I COULD PROVIDE *INSPIRATION...*

...BUT FOR *ME*, THE WAR EXISTED ONLY ON THAT SMALL FARM IN FRANCE, AND THE AIR WE PATROLLED.

OUR DUTY WAS *CLEAR*--OUR ENEMIES *IN FRONT* OF US.

WELCOME HOME BILLY!

THE *HORRORS* WE FACED WERE *FIRST HAND*...

...AND *EVERY DAY.*

TO THEM, THE WAR WAS *IMMENSE*-- AND I WAS A HOMETOWN BOY WHO HAD NOT ONLY SURVIVED, BUT *EXCELLED.*

IN THAT SENSE, I COULD UNDERSTAND MY *IMPORTANCE* TO THEM--NOT AS A SOLDIER, BUT AS A SYMBOL OF *HOPE.*

BUT THIS *STAGE*--THESE *PEOPLE...*

...THEY MAKE ME *UNCOMFORTABLE.*

I'VE HEARD THE MILITARY WANTS TO *KEEP* ME HERE--*STOP* ME FROM GOING BACK TO THE *FRONT...*

...THE THOUGHT IS *TERRIFYING.*

SINCE MY INVESTITURE, I'VE ALREADY WON A SECOND *D.S.O.* AND THE FRENCH *CROIX DE GUERRE.*

BEFORE LEAVING FRANCE, I'D RAISED MY TOTAL TO *FIFTY VICTORIES.*

I'M NOW THE HIGHEST SCORING AIRMAN IN THE *ROYAL FLYING CORPS.*

THE *HUNS* CAN SLEEP EASY FOR *NOW...*

...BUT I WANT *MORE.*

IN EARLY 1918, BILLY BISHOP RETURNED TO FRANCE WITH A NEW SE5 SCOUT AND HIS NEW SQUADRON, "THE FLYING FOXES."

BISHOP EVENTUALLY EARNED AN OFFICIAL TOTAL OF SEVENTY-TWO VICTORIES, THE THIRD HIGHEST IN THE WAR.

AT THAT POINT, BEFORE THE END OF THE WAR, HE WAS FORCED TO RETURN TO CANADA.

IT WAS DECIDED THAT THE EFFECT HIS DEATH COULD HAVE ON CANADIAN MORALE WAS TOO GREAT TO RISK.

ONCE BACK IN CANADA, BISHOP HELPED FORM THE ROYAL CANADIAN AIR FORCE.

IN 1938, HE WAS MADE AN HONORARY AIR MARSHAL, AND WENT ON TO PLAY AN IMPORTANT ROLE IN RECRUITMENT DURING WORLD WAR II.

IN 1956, AIR MARSHAL WILLIAM AVERY BISHOP, V.C., C.B., D.S.O. AND BAR, D.F.C., E.D., DIED IN HIS SLEEP AT THE AGE OF SIXTY-TWO.

ACKNOWLEDGEMENTS

First, I'd like to thank my wife, Sara, for her unwavering kindness, love, and support throughout the creation of *Lone Hawk*. I couldn't have done it without you.

Thanks to Samantha Haywood for her hard work and support in making this book a reality, and without whom this series of graphic novel biographies would not exist.

My thanks to Jeff Lemire, not only for the wonderful foreword he contributed to this book, but also for originally connecting me with Sam and suggesting that I would be a good fit for this series.

I'd like to thank Jennifer Notman, Caitlin Drake, Jonathan Webb, Lynne Missen, and Mary Ann Blair for their tireless efforts, as well as everyone at Penguin Canada who contributed to *Lone Hawk*.

I'm deeply grateful to Kristian Bauthus, whose help and support made all the difference in the long process of creating this book.

Last, I'd like to thank Laura Thomson and the Billy Bishop Museum in Owen Sound for helping me with my research and kindly allowing me to take reference photos that greatly aided in my artwork.